Eighteen Hundred and Eleven

Anna Laetitia Barbauld

Contents

EIGHTEEN HUNDRED AND ELEVEN

BY

Anna Laetitia Barbauld

EIGHTEEN HUNDRED AND ELEVEN,
A POEM.

BY ANNA LÝTITIA BARBAULD.

LONDON:

PRINTED FOR J. JOHNSON AND CO.,
ST. PAUL'S CHURCHYARD.

1812.

PRINTED BY
RICHARD TAYLOR AND CO., SHOE LANE.

EIGHTEEN HUNDRED AND ELEVEN.

Still the loud death drum, thundering from afar,
O'er the vext nations pours the storm of war:
To the stern call still Britain bends her ear,

Feeds the fierce strife, the alternate hope and fear;
Bravely, though vainly, dares to strive with Fate,
And seeks by turns to prop each sinking state.
Colossal Power with overwhelming force   [2]
Bears down each fort of Freedom in its course;
Prostrate she lies beneath the Despot's sway,
While the hushed nations curse him--and obey,

Bounteous in vain, with frantic man at strife,
Glad Nature pours the means--the joys of life;
In vain with orange blossoms scents the gale,
The hills with olives clothes, with corn the vale;
Man calls to Famine, nor invokes in vain,
Disease and Rapine follow in her train;
The tramp of marching hosts disturbs the plough,
The sword, not sickle, reaps the harvest now,
And where the Soldier gleans the scant supply.
The helpless Peasant but retires to die;
No laws his hut from licensed outrage shield,   [3]
And war's least horror is the ensanguined field.

Fruitful in vain, the matron counts with pride
The blooming youths that grace her honoured side;
No son returns to press her widow'd hand,
Her fallen blossoms strew a foreign strand.
--Fruitful in vain, she boasts her virgin race,
Whom cultured arts adorn and gentlest grace;
Defrauded of its homage, Beauty mourns,
And the rose withers on its virgin thorns.

Frequent, some stream obscure, some uncouth name
By deeds of blood is lifted into fame;
Oft o'er the daily page some soft-one bends
To learn the fate of husband, brothers, friends,
Or the spread map with anxious eye explores,   [4]
Its dotted boundaries and penciled shores,
Asks *where* the spot that wrecked her bliss is found,
And learns its name but to detest the sound.

And thinks't thou, Britain, still to sit at ease,
An island Queen amidst thy subject seas,
While the vext billows, in their distant roar,
But soothe thy slumbers, and but kiss thy shore?
To sport in wars, while danger keeps aloof,
Thy grassy turf unbruised by hostile hoof?
So sing thy flatterers; but, Britain, know,
Thou who hast shared the guilt must share the woe.
Nor distant is the hour; low murmurs spread,
And whispered fears, creating what they dread;
Ruin, as with an earthquake shock, is here,   [5]
There, the heart-witherings of unuttered fear,
And that sad death, whence most affection bleeds,
Which sickness, only of the soul, precedes.
Thy baseless wealth dissolves in air away,
Like mists that melt before the morning ray:
No more on crowded mart or busy street
Friends, meeting friends, with cheerful hurry greet;
Sad, on the ground thy princely merchants bend
Their altered looks, and evil days portend,

And fold their arms, and watch with anxious breast
The tempest blackening in the distant West.

Yes, thou must droop; thy Midas dream is o'er;
The golden tide of Commerce leaves thy shore,
Leaves thee to prove the alternate ills that haunt   [6]
Enfeebling Luxury and ghastly Want;
Leaves thee, perhaps, to visit distant lands,
And deal the gifts of Heaven with equal hands.

Yet, O my Country, name beloved, revered,
By every tie that binds the soul endeared,
Whose image to my infant senses came
Mixt with Religion's light and Freedom's holy flame!
If prayers may not avert, if 'tis thy fate
To rank amongst the names that once were great,
Not like the dim cold Crescent shalt thou fade,
Thy debt to Science and the Muse unpaid;
Thine are the laws surrounding states revere,
Thine the full harvest of the mental year,
Thine the bright stars in Glory's sky that shine,   [7]
And arts that make it life to live are thine.
If westward streams the light that leaves thy shores,
Still from thy lamp the streaming radiance pours.
Wide spreads thy race from Ganges to the pole,
O'er half the western world thy accents roll:
Nations beyond the Apalachian hills
Thy hand has planted and thy spirit fills:
Soon as their gradual progress shall impart

The finer sense of morals and of art,
Thy stores of knowledge the new states shall know,
And think thy thoughts, and with thy fancy glow;
Thy Lockes, thy Paleys shall instruct their youth,
Thy leading star direct their search for truth;
Beneath the spreading Platan's tent-like shade,   [8]
Or by Missouri's rushing waters laid,
"Old father Thames" shall be the Poets' theme,
Of Hagley's woods the enamoured virgin dream,
And Milton's tones the raptured ear enthrall,
Mixt with the roar of Niagara's fall;
In Thomson's glass the ingenuous youth shall learn
A fairer face of Nature to discern;
Nor of the Bards that swept the British lyre
Shall fade one laurel, or one note expire.
Then, loved Joanna, to admiring eyes
Thy storied groups in scenic pomp shall rise;
Their high soul'd strains and Shakespear's noble rage
Shall with alternate passion shake the stage.
Some youthful Basil from thy moral lay   [9]
With stricter hand his fond desires shall sway;
Some Ethwald, as the fleeting shadows pass,
Start at his likeness in the mystic glass;
The tragic Muse resume her just controul,
With pity and with terror purge the soul,
While wide o'er transatlantic realms thy name
Shall live in light, and gather *all* its fame.

Where wanders Fancy down the lapse of years

Shedding o'er imaged woes untimely tears?
Fond moody Power! as hopes--as fears prevail,
She longs, or dreads, to lift the awful veil,
On visions of delight now loves to dwell,
Now hears the shriek of woe or Freedom's knell:
Perhaps, she says, long ages past away,   [10]
And set in western waves our closing day,
Night, Gothic night, again may shade the plains
Where Power is seated, and where Science reigns;
England, the seat of arts, be only known
By the gray ruin and the mouldering stone;
That Time may tear the garland from her brow,
And Europe sit in dust, as Asia now.

Yet then the ingenuous youth whom Fancy fires
With pictured glories of illustrious sires,
With duteous zeal their pilgrimage shall take
From the blue mountains, or Ontario's lake,
With fond adoring steps to press the sod
By statesmen, sages, poets, heroes trod;
On Isis' banks to draw inspiring air,   [11]
From Runnymede to send the patriot's prayer;
In pensive thought, where Cam's slow waters wind,
To meet those shades that ruled the realms of mind;
In silent halls to sculptured marbles bow,
And hang fresh wreaths round Newton's awful brow.
Oft shall they seek some peasant's homely shed,
Who toils, unconscious of the mighty dead,
To ask where Avon's winding waters stray,

And thence a knot of wild flowers bear away;
Anxious enquire where Clarkson, friend of man,
Or all-accomplished Jones his race began;
If of the modest mansion aught remains
Where Heaven and Nature prompted Cowper's strains;
Where Roscoe, to whose patriot breast belong   [12]
The Roman virtue and the Tuscan song,
Led Ceres to the black and barren moor
Where Ceres never gained a wreath before[1]:
With curious search their pilgrim steps shall rove
By many a ruined tower and proud alcove,
Shall listen for those strains that soothed of yore
Thy rock, stern Skiddaw, and thy fall, Lodore;
Feast with Dun Edin's classic brow their sight,
And visit "Melross by the pale moonlight."

But who their mingled feelings shall pursue
When London's faded glories rise to view?
The mighty city, which by every road,   [13]
In floods of people poured itself abroad;
Ungirt by walls, irregularly great,
No jealous drawbridge, and no closing gate;
Whose merchants (such the state which commerce brings)
Sent forth their mandates to dependant kings:
Streets, where the turban'd Moslem, bearded Jew,
And woolly Afric, met the brown Hindu;
Where through each vein spontaneous plenty flowed,
Where Wealth enjoyed, and Charity bestowed.
Pensive and thoughtful shall the wanderers greet

Each splendid square, and still, untrodden street;
Or of some crumbling turret, mined by time,
The broken stair with perilous step shall climb,
Thence stretch their view the wide horizon round,   [14]
By scattered hamlets trace its antient bound,
And, choked no more with fleets, fair Thames survey
Through reeds and sedge pursue his idle way.

With throbbing bosoms shall the wanderers tread
The hallowed mansions of the silent dead,
Shall enter the long isle and vaulted dome
Where Genius and where Valour find a home;
Awe-struck, midst chill sepulchral marbles breathe,
Where all above is still, as all beneath;
Bend at each antique shrine, and frequent turn
To clasp with fond delight some sculptured urn,
The ponderous mass of Johnson's form to greet,
Or breathe the prayer at Howard's sainted feet.

Perhaps some Briton, in whose musing mind   [15]
Those ages live which Time has cast behind,
To every spot shall lead his wondering guests
On whose known site the beam of glory rests:
Here Chatham's eloquence in thunder broke,
Here Fox persuaded, or here Garrick spoke;
Shall boast how Nelson, fame and death in view,
To wonted victory led his ardent crew,
In England's name enforced, with loftiest tone[2],
Their duty,--and too well fulfilled his own:

How gallant Moore[3], as ebbing life dissolved,
But hoped his country had his fame absolved.
Or call up sages whose capacious mind   [16]
Left in its course a track of light behind;
Point where mute crowds on Davy's lips reposed,
And Nature's coyest secrets were disclosed;
Join with their Franklin, Priestley's injured name,
Whom, then, each continent shall proudly claim.

Oft shall the strangers turn their eager feet
The rich remains of antient art to greet,
The pictured walls with critic eye explore,
And Reynolds be what Raphael was before.
On spoils from every clime their eyes shall gaze,
Ýgyptian granites and the Etruscan vase;
And when midst fallen London, they survey
The stone where Alexander's ashes lay,
Shall own with humbled pride the lesson just   [17]
By Time's slow finger written in the dust.

There walks a Spirit o'er the peopled earth,
Secret his progress is, unknown his birth;
Moody and viewless as the changing wind,
No force arrests his foot, no chains can bind;
Where'er he turns, the human brute awakes,
And, roused to better life, his sordid hut forsakes:
He thinks, he reasons, glows with purer fires,
Feels finer wants, and burns with new desires:
Obedient Nature follows where he leads;

The steaming marsh is changed to fruitful meads;
The beasts retire from man's asserted reign,
And prove his kingdom was not given in vain.
Then from its bed is drawn the ponderous ore,   [18]
Then Commerce pours her gifts on every shore,
Then Babel's towers and terrassed gardens rise,
And pointed obelisks invade the skies;
The prince commands, in Tyrian purple drest,
And Ýgypt's virgins weave the linen vest.
Then spans the graceful arch the roaring tide,
And stricter bounds the cultured fields divide.
Then kindles Fancy, then expands the heart,
Then blow the flowers of Genius and of Art;
Saints, Heroes, Sages, who the land adorn,
Seem rather to descend than to be born;
Whilst History, midst the rolls consigned to fame,
With pen of adamant inscribes their name.

The Genius now forsakes the favoured shore,   [19]
And hates, capricious, what he loved before;
Then empires fall to dust, then arts decay,
And wasted realms enfeebled despots sway;
Even Nature's changed; without his fostering smile
Ophir no gold, no plenty yields the Nile;
The thirsty sand absorbs the useless rill,
And spotted plagues from putrid fens distill.
In desert solitudes then Tadmor sleeps,
Stern Marius then o'er fallen Carthage weeps;
Then with enthusiast love the pilgrim roves

To seek his footsteps in forsaken groves,
Explores the fractured arch, the ruined tower,
Those limbs disjointed of gigantic power;
Still at each step he dreads the adder's sting,   [20]
The Arab's javelin, or the tiger's spring;
With doubtful caution treads the echoing ground.
And asks where Troy or Babylon is found.

And now the vagrant Power no more detains
The vale of Tempe, or Ausonian plains;
Northward he throws the animating ray,
O'er Celtic nations bursts the mental day:
And, as some playful child the mirror turns,
Now here now there the moving lustre burns;
Now o'er his changeful fancy more prevail
Batavia's dykes than Arno's purple vale,
And stinted suns, and rivers bound with frost,
Than Enna's plains or Baia's viny coast;
Venice the Adriatic weds in vain,   [21]
And Death sits brooding o'er Campania's plain;
O'er Baltic shores and through Hercynian groves,
Stirring the soul, the mighty impulse moves;
Art plies his tools, arid Commerce spreads her sail,
And wealth is wafted in each shifting gale.
The sons of Odin tread on Persian looms,
And Odin's daughters breathe distilled perfumes;
Loud minstrel Bards, in Gothic halls, rehearse
The Runic rhyme, and "build the lofty verse:"
The Muse, whose liquid notes were wont to swell

To the soft breathings of the' Ýolian shell,
Submits, reluctant, to the harsher tone,
And scarce believes the altered voice her own.
And now, where Cæsar saw with proud disdain   [22]
The wattled hut and skin of azure stain,
Corinthian columns rear their graceful forms,
And light varandas brave the wintry storms,
While British tongues the fading fame prolong
Of Tully's eloquence and Maro's song.
Where once Bonduca whirled the scythed car,
And the fierce matrons raised the shriek of war,
Light forms beneath transparent muslins float,
And tutored voices swell the artful note.
Light-leaved acacias and the shady plane
And spreading cedar grace the woodland reign;
While crystal walls the tenderer plants confine,
The fragrant orange and the nectared pine;
The Syrian grape there hangs her rich festoons,   [23]
Nor asks for purer air, or brighter noons:
Science and Art urge on the useful toil,
New mould a climate and create the soil,
Subdue the rigour of the northern Bear,
O'er polar climes shed aromatic air,
On yielding Nature urge their new demands,
And ask not gifts but tribute at her hands.

London exults:--on London Art bestows
Her summer ices and her winter rose;
Gems of the East her mural crown adorn,

And Plenty at her feet pours forth her horn;
While even the exiles her just laws disclaim,
People a continent, and build a name:
August she sits, and with extended hands   [24]
Holds forth the book of life to distant lands.

But fairest flowers expand but to decay;
The worm is in thy core, thy glories pass away;
Arts, arms and wealth destroy the fruits they bring;
Commerce, like beauty, knows no second spring.
Crime walks thy streets, Fraud earns her unblest bread,
O'er want and woe thy gorgeous robe is spread,
And angel charities in vain oppose:
With grandeur's growth the mass of misery grows.
For see,--to other climes the Genius soars,
He turns from Europe's desolated shores;
And lo, even now, midst mountains wrapt in storm,
On Andes' heights he shrouds his awful form;
On Chimborazo's summits treads sublime,   [25]
Measuring in lofty thought the march of Time;
Sudden he calls:--"'Tis now the hour!" he cries,
Spreads his broad hand, and bids the nations rise.
La Plata hears amidst her torrents' roar,
Potosi hears it, as she digs the ore:
Ardent, the Genius fans the noble strife,
And pours through feeble souls a higher life,
Shouts to the mingled tribes from sea to sea,
And swears--Thy world, Columbus, shall be free.

THE END.

Notes:

[1] The Historian of the age of Leo has brought into cultivation the extensive tract of Chatmoss.

[2] Every reader will recollect the sublime telegraphic dispatch, "England expects every man to do his duty."

[3] "I hope England will be satisfied," were the last words of General Moore.

The Codes Of Hammurabi And Moses
W. W. Davies

QTY

The discovery of the Hammurabi Code is one of the greatest achievements of archaeology, and is of paramount interest, not only to the student of the Bible, but also to all those interested in ancient history...

Religion   ISBN: *1-59462-338-4*   Pages:132

MSRP $12.95

The Theory of Moral Sentiments
Adam Smith

QTY

This work from 1749. contains original theories of conscience amd moral judgment and it is the foundation for systemof morals.

Philosophy ISBN: *1-59462-777-0*   Pages:536

MSRP $19.95

Jessica's First Prayer
Hesba Stretton

QTY

In a screened and secluded corner of one of the many railway-bridges which span the streets of London there could be seen a few years ago, from five o'clock every morning until half past eight, a tidily set-out coffee-stall, consisting of a trestle and board, upon which stood two large tin cans, with a small fire of charcoal burning under each so as to keep the coffee boiling during the early hours of the morning when the work-people were thronging into the city on their way to their daily toil...

Childrens   ISBN: *1-59462-373-2*

Pages:84

MSRP $9.95

My Life and Work
Henry Ford

QTY

Henry Ford revolutionized the world with his implementation of mass production for the Model T automobile. Gain valuable business insight into his life and work with his own auto-biography... "We have only started on our development of our country we have not as yet, with all our talk of wonderful progress, done more than scratch the surface. The progress has been wonderful enough but..."

Biographies/   ISBN: *1-59462-198-5*

Pages:300

MSRP $21.95

The Art of Cross-Examination
Francis Wellman

QTY

I presume it is the experience of every author, after his first book is published upon an important subject, to be almost overwhelmed with a wealth of ideas and illustrations which could readily have been included in his book, and which to his own mind, at least, seem to make a second edition inevitable. Such certainly was the case with me; and when the first edition had reached its sixth impression in five months, I rejoiced to learn that it seemed to my publishers that the book had met with a sufficiently favorable reception to justify a second and considerably enlarged edition. ..

Pages:412

Reference   **ISBN: *1-59462-647-2***   *MSRP $19.95*

On the Duty of Civil Disobedience
Henry David Thoreau

QTY

Thoreau wrote his famous essay, On the Duty of Civil Disobedience, as a protest against an unjust but popular war and the immoral but popular institution of slave-owning. He did more than write—he declined to pay his taxes, and was hauled off to gaol in consequence. Who can say how much this refusal of his hastened the end of the war and of slavery ?

Law   **ISBN: *1-59462-747-9***   **Pages:48**

MSRP $7.45

Dream Psychology Psychoanalysis for Beginners
Sigmund Freud

QTY

Sigmund Freud, born Sigismund Schlomo Freud (May 6, 1856 - September 23, 1939), was a Jewish-Austrian neurologist and psychiatrist who co-founded the psychoanalytic school of psychology. Freud is best known for his theories of the unconscious mind, especially involving the mechanism of repression; his redefinition of sexual desire as mobile and directed towards a wide variety of objects; and his therapeutic techniques, especially his understanding of transference in the therapeutic relationship and the presumed value of dreams as sources of insight into unconscious desires.

Pages:196

Psychology   **ISBN: *1-59462-905-6***   *MSRP $15.45*

The Miracle of Right Thought
Orison Swett Marden

QTY

Believe with all of your heart that you will do what you were made to do. When the mind has once formed the habit of holding cheerful, happy, prosperous pictures, it will not be easy to form the opposite habit. It does not matter how improbable or how far away this realization may see, or how dark the prospects may be, if we visualize them as best we can, as vividly as possible, hold tenaciously to them and vigorously struggle to attain them, they will gradually become actualized, realized in the life. But a desire, a longing without endeavor, a yearning abandoned or held indifferently will vanish without realization.

Pages:360

Self Help   **ISBN: *1-59462-644-8***   *MSRP $25.45*

www.**bookjungle**.com *email: sales@bookjungle.com fax: 630-214-0564 mail: Book Jungle PO Box 2226 Champaign, IL 61825*

QTY

The Rosicrucian Cosmo-Conception Mystic Christianity *by Max Heindel*   ISBN: *1-59462-188-8*   **$38.95**
The Rosicrucian Cosmo-conception is not dogmatic, neither does it appeal to any other authority than the reason of the student. It is: not controversial, but is: sent forth in the, hope that it may help to clear...   *New Age/Religion Pages 646*

Abandonment To Divine Providence *by Jean-Pierre de Caussade*   ISBN: *1-59462-228-0*   **$25.95**
"The Rev. Jean Pierre de Caussade was one of the most remarkable spiritual writers of the Society of Jesus in France in the 18th Century. His death took place at Toulouse in 1751. His works have gone through many editions and have been republished...   *Inspirational/Religion Pages 400*

Mental Chemistry *by Charles Haanel*   ISBN: *1-59462-192-6*   **$23.95**
Mental Chemistry allows the change of material conditions by combining and appropriately utilizing the power of the mind. Much like applied chemistry creates something new and unique out of careful combinations of chemicals the mastery of mental chemistry...   *New Age Pages 354*

The Letters of Robert Browning and Elizabeth Barret Barrett 1845-1846 vol II   ISBN: *1-59462-193-4*   **$35.95**
by Robert Browning and Elizabeth Barrett   *Biographies Pages 596*

Gleanings In Genesis (volume I) *by Arthur W. Pink*   ISBN: *1-59462-130-6*   **$27.45**
Appropriately has Genesis been termed "the seed plot of the Bible" for in it we have, in germ form, almost all of the great doctrines which are afterwards fully developed in the books of Scripture which follow...   *Religion/Inspirational Pages 420*

The Master Key *by L. W. de Laurence*   ISBN: *1-59462-001-6*   **$30.95**
In no branch of human knowledge has there been a more lively increase of the spirit of research during the past few years than in the study of Psychology, Concentration and Mental Discipline. The requests for authentic lessons in Thought Control, Mental Discipline and...   *New Age/Business Pages 422*

The Lesser Key Of Solomon Goetia *by L. W. de Laurence*   ISBN: *1-59462-092-X*   **$9.95**
This translation of the first book of the "Lernegton" which is now for the first time made accessible to students of Talismanic Magic was done, after careful collation and edition, from numerous Ancient Manuscripts in Hebrew, Latin, and French...   *New Age/Occult Pages 92*

Rubaiyat Of Omar Khayyam *by Edward Fitzgerald*   ISBN:*1-59462-332-5*   **$13.95**
Edward Fitzgerald, whom the world has already learned, in spite of his own efforts to remain within the shadow of anonymity, to look upon as one of the rarest poets of the century, was born at Bredfield, in Suffolk, on the 31st of March, 1809. He was the third son of John Purcell...   *Music Pages 172*

Ancient Law *by Henry Maine*   ISBN: *1-59462-128-4*   **$29.95**
The chief object of the following pages is to indicate some of the earliest ideas of mankind, as they are reflected in Ancient Law, and to point out the relation of those ideas to modern thought.   *Religion/History Pages 452*

Far-Away Stories *by William J. Locke*   ISBN: *1-59462-129-2*   **$19.45**
"Good wine needs no bush, but a collection of mixed vintages does. And this book is just such a collection. Some of the stories I do not want to remain buried for ever in the museum files of dead magazine-numbers an author's not unpardonable vanity..."   *Fiction Pages 272*

Life of David Crockett *by David Crockett*   ISBN: *1-59462-250-7*   **$27.45**
"Colonel David Crockett was one of the most remarkable men of the times in which he lived. Born in humble life, but gifted with a strong will, an indomitable courage, and unremitting perseverance...   *Biographies/New Age Pages 424*

Lip-Reading *by Edward Nitchie*   ISBN: *1-59462-206-X*   **$25.95**
Edward B. Nitchie, founder of the New York School for the Hard of Hearing, now the Nitchie School of Lip-Reading, Inc, wrote "LIP-READING Principles and Practice". The development and perfecting of this meritorious work on lip-reading was an undertaking...   *How-to Pages 400*

A Handbook of Suggestive Therapeutics, Applied Hypnotism, Psychic Science   ISBN: *1-59462-214-0*   **$24.95**
by Henry Munro   *Health/New Age/Health/Self-help Pages 376*

A Doll's House: and Two Other Plays *by Henrik Ibsen*   ISBN: *1-59462-112-8*   **$19.95**
Henrik Ibsen created this classic when in revolutionary 1848 Rome. Introducing some striking concepts in playwriting for the realist genre, this play has been studied the world over.   *Fiction/Classics/Plays 308*

The Light of Asia *by sir Edwin Arnold*   ISBN: *1-59462-204-3*   **$13.95**
In this poetic masterpiece, Edwin Arnold describes the life and teachings of Buddha. The man who was to become known as Buddha to the world was born as Prince Gautama of India but he rejected the worldly riches and abandoned the reigns of power when...   *Religion/History/Biographies Pages 170*

The Complete Works of Guy de Maupassant *by Guy de Maupassant*   ISBN: *1-59462-157-8*   **$16.95**
"For days and days, nights and nights, I had dreamed of that first kiss which was to consecrate our engagement, and I knew not on what spot I should put my lips..."   *Fiction/Classics Pages 240*

The Art of Cross-Examination *by Francis L. Wellman*   ISBN: *1-59462-309-0*   **$26.95**
Written by a renowned trial lawyer, Wellman imparts his experience and uses case studies to explain how to use psychology to extract desired information through questioning.   *How-to/Science/Reference Pages 408*

Answered or Unanswered? *by Louisa Vaughan*   ISBN: *1-59462-248-5*   **$10.95**
Miracles of Faith in China   *Religion Pages 112*

The Edinburgh Lectures on Mental Science (1909) *by Thomas*   ISBN: *1-59462-008-3*   **$11.95**
This book contains the substance of a course of lectures recently given by the writer in the Queen Street Hall, Edinburgh. Its purpose is to indicate the Natural Principles governing the relation between Mental Action and Material Conditions...   *New Age/Psychology Pages 148*

Ayesha *by H. Rider Haggard*   ISBN: *1-59462-301-5*   **$24.95**
Verily and indeed it is the unexpected that happens! Probably if there was one person upon the earth from whom the Editor of this, and of a certain previous history, did not expect to hear again...   *Classics Pages 380*

Ayala's Angel *by Anthony Trollope*   ISBN: *1-59462-352-X*   **$29.95**
The two girls were both pretty, but Lucy who was twenty-one who supposed to be simple and comparatively unattractive, whereas Ayala was credited, as her Bombwhat romantic name might show, with poetic charm and a taste for romance. Ayala when her father died was nineteen...   *Fiction Pages 484*

The American Commonwealth *by James Bryce*   ISBN: *1-59462-286-8*   **$34.45**
An interpretation of American democratic political theory. It examines political mechanics and society from the perspective of Scotsman James Bryce   *Politics Pages 572*

Stories of the Pilgrims *by Margaret P. Pumphrey*   ISBN: *1-59462-116-0*   **$17.95**
This book explores pilgrims religious oppression in England as well as their escape to Holland and eventual crossing to America on the Mayflower, and their early days in New England...   *History Pages 268*

QTY

The Fasting Cure *by Sinclair Upton* ISBN: *1-59462-222-1* **$13.95**
In the Cosmopolitan Magazine for May, 1910, and in the Contemporary Review (London) for April, 1910, I published an article dealing with my experiences in fasting. I have written a great many magazine articles, but never one which attracted so much attention... New Age/Self Help/Health Pages 164 ☐

Hebrew Astrology *by Sepharial* ISBN: *1-59462-308-2* **$13.45**
In these days of advanced thinking it is a matter of common observation that we have left many of the old landmarks behind and that we are now pressing forward to greater heights and to a wider horizon than that which represented the mind-content of our progenitors... Astrology Pages 144 ☐

Thought Vibration or The Law of Attraction in the Thought World ISBN: *1-59462-127-6* **$12.95**
by William Walker Atkinson Psychology/Religion Pages 144 ☐

Optimism *by Helen Keller* ISBN: *1-59462-108-X* **$15.95**
Helen Keller was blind, deaf, and mute since 19 months old, yet famously learned how to overcome these handicaps, communicate with the world, and spread her lectures promoting optimism. An inspiring read for everyone... Biographies/Inspirational Pages 84 ☐

Sara Crewe *by Frances Burnett* ISBN: *1-59462-360-0* **$9.45**
In the first place, Miss Minchin lived in London. Her home was a large, dull, tall one, in a large, dull square, where all the houses were alike, and all the sparrows were alike, and where all the door-knockers made the same heavy sound... Childrens/Classic Pages 88 ☐

The Autobiography of Benjamin Franklin *by Benjamin Franklin* ISBN: *1-59462-135-7* **$24.95**
The Autobiography of Benjamin Franklin has probably been more extensively read than any other American historical work, and no other book of its kind has had such ups and downs of fortune. Franklin lived for many years in England, where he was agent... Biographies/History Pages 332 ☐

Name	
Email	
Telephone	
Address	
City, State ZIP	

☐ **Credit Card**   ☐ **Check / Money Order**

Credit Card Number	
Expiration Date	
Signature	

Please Mail to: Book Jungle
PO Box 2226
Champaign, IL 61825
or Fax to: *630-214-0564*

ORDERING INFORMATION

web*: www.bookjungle.com*
email*: sales@bookjungle.com*
fax*: 630-214-0564*
mail*: Book Jungle PO Box 2226 Champaign, IL 61825*
or PayPal *to sales@bookjungle.com*

Please contact us for bulk discounts

DIRECT-ORDER TERMS

**20% Discount if You Order
Two or More Books**
Free Domestic Shipping!
Accepted: Master Card, Visa,
Discover, American Express